A Bedtime Yarn

Nicola Winstanley

Olivia Chin Mueller

tundra

Tundra Books, an imprint of Penguin Random House Canada Young Readers, a
Penguin Random House Company

Library and Archives Canada Cataloguing in Publication

Winstanley, Nicola, author
A bedtime yarn / Nicola Winstanley ; Olivia Chin Mueller, illustrator.

Issued in print and electronic formats.
ISBN 978-1-101-91808-1 (hardback).—ISBN 978-1-101-91810-4 (epub)

    I. Mueller, Olivia Chin, illustrator II. Title.

PS8645.I57278B43 2017   jC813'.6   C2016-906826-9
                                                  C2016-906827-7

Published simultaneously in the United States of America by Tundra Books of
Northern New York, an imprint of Penguin Random House Canada Young Readers,
a Penguin Random House Company

Library of Congress Control Number: 2016956548

Edited by Samantha Swenson
Designed by Jennifer Griffiths
The artwork in this book was created digitally.
The text was set in Carre Noir.

Printed and bound in China

www.penguinrandomhouse.ca

1 2 3 4 5   21 20 19 18 17

For Joanna and Chris, with all my love
—*Nicola*

To mom and dad, thank you so much for everything!
—*Livi*

O nce upon a time, in a village
by the sea, there lived a little bear
named Frankie. He slept in his own little
room, in his own little bed, and fell asleep
each night listening to the faint *click, click*
of his mother's knitting needles as a ball
of yarn unravelled in his paws.

His mother would sit in her cozy chair by the fire as she worked the other end of the wool, listening to music with the cat on her knee.

Every few days the ball of yarn would shrink to nothing, and Frankie's mother would give him a new one. Each ball was as soft and smooth as the one before, and each ball was a different color.

Frankie's favorite yarn was
a smooth,
morning-sky blue.
But every color had a story.

One night,
Frankie held a
cool, foamy sea-green
that led him to deep
underwater caverns.

On another, he bravely
gripped a bright
orange-and-black striped
tiger's tail . . .

and later he
wrapped his
fingers around
a flickering
red flame that
didn't hurt
him at all.

Once he held
an ice-cold
ball of snow.

And once he
brushed his cheek
with a damp,
gray fog.

He cupped his
palms around
turquoise-and-cream
speckled eggs . . .

and gently
patted a
marmalade
kitten.

He smelled the tangy scent of the bright
green lawn where he played barefoot in the summer.

And he sniffed

the yellow dandelions

that covered the grass

in the spring,

and sneezed!

The day before his birthday,
his mother gave him a rich brown that
made Frankie hungry for cake.

Without the yarn, Frankie had been afraid of sleep.
He didn't know where the darkness would take him,
and if it took him too far, how he would ever get
back. Holding the yarn, Frankie felt anchored like
the boats in the bay, bobbing and drifting, but not
floating away.

Frankie's mother would not
show him what the *click, click*
of her needles was making.

"A surprise," said his mother.
"It will be finished when you
are ready to let go of your last
ball of yarn."

Night after night, the vivid colors passed
through Frankie's fingers as he slept. But over
time, his curiosity grew with his legs, until,
after many months, it overcame his fear.

"Mama, I am getting to be a big boy."

"Yes?" said his mother.

"I'm still a little bit afraid, but I'm
ready to let go of the yarn. I want to
see what we've made."

"Then I think it's time for one last ball,"
said his mother.

That night, Frankie held on to the invisible yarn his mother had placed in his paw and closed his eyes.

The next morning, just as the sun
began to shine through his window,
Frankie woke and stretched and looked
down to see that he was covered in a
blanket that shimmered and rippled with
every color he had held in his hand.

The colors ran together in surprising shapes and patterns, as they do in dreams. Frankie gazed at the blanket, and in the colors of its fabric he saw the sky and the sea; tigers and flames; bright white snow and sweet green grass dotted with dandelions; delicate eggs; fluffy kittens; and sweet chocolate cake.

Frankie saw that no matter how
far away he floated in his dreams,
this blanket, like a magic carpet,
would always bring him back to
his own little bed.

That night, Frankie kissed his
mother, snuggled under his blanket
and fell asleep, his paws empty of yarn
and his head full of all the wonderful
dreams he and his mother had
knitted up together.